GOING WITH THE FLOW

Text: Andrea Pfaucht
              Fabia Feuerabendt

Cover: Marita Mueller

© Andrea Pfaucht, Fabia Feuerabendt

Herstellung und Verlag:
Books on Demand GmbH, Norderstedt

ISBN 978-3-8482-0783-1

März 2012

Thank You ...

... Soidog Foundation, their friends and supporters for your tireless effort, which saved more than thousand animals from certain death....

The returnes of this book are intended for Thailand 's soidogs.

www.soidog.org

Let the water flood your house.

Don`t let your mind get flooded with suffering...

Phra Sabchoo

Autumn in Upper Franconia

It is a typical autumn day in a small town in Upper Franconia, 15 degrees Celsius, cloudy and drizzling. The time of the day suggests that the daily walky is starting soon.

Baby Balou, a small French Bulldog, is standing in the backyard door, inspects the weather and tries to convince her human-mom -with a face that only bulldogs can have- that it is impossible to put a paw outside this door. It's way too cold! Killer weather!

Human-mom is just sitting in front of the telly. She gets up and goes to the door, but after the first step she stops instantly and turns back to the telly. Something is different. No attempts to convince Baby to go for a walk. No despicable arguments to make the walky more enjoyable. Baby has new hopes and wonders: "Should the walk really be cancelled because of the cold-wet weather?"

What has happened?

Mom turns pale and stares at the telly.

"Baby, this is not good at all! Your doggy-mom and sister are getting wet paws. Very wet paws!"

"Woof. "

Luckily, the unpleasant walky really seems to be cancelled for now. However, Baby Balou does not understand why human-mom is so stressed out, just because doggy-mom Tequila's paws are getting wet? After all, doggy-mom loves playing in the water and swimming is her greatest passion, doggy-mom's greatest passion, Baby is not so fond of water though. Besides, doggy-mom and doggy-

sister Ginger are living in Bangkok, Thailand. Over there it is cozy and warm, so one might dare to put a paw into the water.

But human-mom is still petrified and stares at the screen.

"Woof, what's up mom?"

"Baby, Thailand is being flooded by heavy monsoon rains. Over there it is difficult for your doggy-mom and her two and four-legged friends, even with life-jackets."

The water has not reached Bangkok yet, but if the floodwaters reach Lisa's and Phillip's house in the northern part of the capital, it will have nothing in common with a private swimming-pool for bulldogs.

This is much better than going for a walk. Baby Balou prefers dreaming of her family in Bangkok.

Lak Si

In Thailand it is raining. It is the heaviest rainy season after 50 years. Huge parts of the country have already been flooded, industrial estates have been inundated and the huts of the poorest people are floating away.

"The capital is at risk now", the news reports. "The situation is really disastrous, especially in the north."

While the elevated roads in Bangkok are still navigable...

... low lying roads are becoming streams.

Lisa and Phillip are living in the northern part of the capital, in the Lak si district. Ming-Ming their kitty and several dogs are part of their family. Tequila, Baby Balou's mom is a black French bulldog with a white bib. Additionally: Baby's sister Ginger, Cane Corso Massimo, Malinois Leki, Thai-Ridgeback Emma as well as the soi dog-sisters Sonnenschein and Windhund. They all trust and adore the German couple and follow them everywhere.

Mood in Upper Franconia

Within a second everything has turned upside down in the small town in Upper Franconia. What is going on in Thailand? - Thailand, the land of smiles, sunshine and people full of Buddhist calmness who approach you with peacefulness – even in the worst moments. How are the two young Germans doing? They left the Franconian province six years ago in order to volunteer as animal activists and then decided to make their home in former Siam.

Baby's human-mom gets more and more anxious and reaches for the phone.

No connection!

Damn!

She starts searching Google for information.

16

No news.

She can only read what the news has just told.

Even though Baby suspects that something is different today, she is happy about the cancelled walky in the cold rain. She has no clue about the dangers her doggy-family is in. Actually, this is a good thing, since excitement and stress usually upset her tummy.

Visiting Baby's sister

A play-date is scheduled for Baby, her other doggy-sister Pepper and a boxer named Arthus – no, he is not related to the Klitschko brothers - but a four-legged one! Their owners live in an even smaller town in Upper Franconia. Back in the days when Baby was small and her human-mom a doggy-newbie these two experienced dog people were always helpful to her.

Human-mom thinks: "Yes, visiting them is a good idea. Maybe they know more, can give an all clear?"

"Hi! Have you got news from Lisa and Phillip? "

"Nope, why? News? A new puppy? "

"Rising water! "

"What? Water? What kind of water? "

"Flooding! Thailand is drowning! "

"What? "

"Yes. Thailand is flooded. And the floodwater mass is moving towards Bangkok. "

"But, Lisa and Phillip are living there! And Tequila. And Ginger. And....."

"Exactly. And they are threatened by the rising waters!"

Meanwhile Baby and Arthus are frolicking on the floor, slobbering, purring and cooing. Baby is enjoying the big strong pup.

When Baby and Arthus meet there is no holding back...

Pepper ignores the two lovers and moves to the telly, it seems that she understands that the news is reporting about the further rising of the water levels in Asia. The flood will probably put an end to Tequila's joy of splashing in waters.

The worries among the two-legged ones grow.

Calling Bangkok

The humans wonder: "What is the time difference between Upper Franconia and Thailand? Fife hours? Six hours? So, calling someone in Thailand now should be an acceptable time over there."

Ring-tuut-ring...

"Hello. Lisa speaking."

Thank God! They are alive. And do not sound desperate at all.

"Yes. Ehm hello. It's me. Ehh Baby. Ehh no, yes..."

"Hi. Good to hear from you. How are you doing?"

"What? What do you mean? How are we doing?

How are you doing? This is way more important!"

"Fine"

"What? Fine? What do you mean with fine?"

"Well, it means: good. Really good, compared to so many others... We are doing really fine. We have been spared from the flooding so far."

Wham! Many, many rocks are falling from Baby's human-mom's shoulders, she is relieved. However, she cannot understand how someone can stay so relaxed in such a disaster.

Bangkok

Following the strongest monsoon rains in recent history the waters take over Thailand, slowly but constantly, the floods are moving towards Bangkok. Right through Lak si there runs the channel Klong Prem, by now it is overflowing its banks. The distance between Lisa's and Phillip's house and the klong is about 800 meters. The situation in and around Bangkok is starting to escalate. Grocery stores are sold out, ATMs are empty, some subway stations had to be closed.

Bangkok's population is preparing for the worst, supermarkets are empty.

In last hope, in order to avoid the worst, people are pulling walls up in front of their doors and gates, piling up sandbags, installing pumps. Fortunately, the power supply has not been affected so far. However, the tap water supply has been contaminated. In several districts the tab water has turned smelly brownish-yellow.

Lisa, Phillip and their four-legged family members can enjoy the luxury of a two-storey house. This means that anything which is mobile has to be brought upstairs. The most important belongings of their neighbors find a dry place there, too. Clean drinking water and food is also stored up there, together with food for the own animals as well as several other feral soidogs. The refrigerator and everything else that cannot be moved upstairs is put on stalks.

Cars are parked on bridges and highways; in Bangkok several evacuation centers are prepared, for example Thammasart University, Phillip's university and Don Mueang airport. However, both locations are at high risk of being inundated now, they are surrounded by water.

Everything of value and importance is brought upstairs. Meanwhile, Ginger and Tequila are taking a last fitting of their life jackets.

Even though the atmosphere in the Thai metropolis is not as relaxed and smooth as usual, Lisa and Phillip are admiring the attitude and sticking together of the people. It is unbelievable how hands on initiative the people are showing. Everybody, even those that have to deal with their own flood related problems, are helping each other out. The offered help is versatile; there are donations of goods and services, preparation and distribution of food in the rescue shelters. Packages with food, drinking water and other necessities are prepared and distributed to those who stayed behind in their inundated houses. As far as possible people are helping each other out with transportation.

For now schools and universities are closed, office workers in Bangkok receive extra holidays in order to take care of important things and to be able to give a helping hand where it is crucial.

Tempeldogs

Lisa, who is currently working on her doctorate, is forced to take a break. Besides her academic activities she is busy volunteering in animal welfare with a lot of commitment. The officially recognized organization *Soi Dog Rescue Foundation* is run solely by volunteers from all around the world: Thailand, the Netherlands, Australia and Switzerland. During common day-to-day life they have made it their duty to diminish rabies among the animals and to provide a life worth living for the countless soi dogs and cats. They catch the sometimes feral animals, sterilize and vaccinate them, provide necessary medical attention and then release them back to their territories.

Now they are flooded with new duties. People who were evacuated from the water masses often were not able or not allowed to bring their beloved pets along. They had to leave them behind in uncertainty.

The monks in the temple Wat Suankaew, located in Nonthaburi province and adjacent to western Bangkok, are helping these poor creatures. They take in all sorts of animals that otherwise had no chance to survive, provide food and shelter as long as necessary.

Within a very short period of time more than 1,000 animals have accumulated there.

However, the flood does not spare the temple and is approaching quickly. Soon the temple is surrounded by water.

Evacuating Wat Suankaew

More than 1,000 animals have stranded there. At the worst, without any help, they would be doomed to turn into cadavers floating through Bangkok. Hundreds of volunteers are concerned, they are working hard on alleviating the suffering of these animals.

They start their journey to the temple on a truck, other vehicles cannot get through the rapidly rising water any longer, taking styrofoam-boxes, small boats and a catching-net with them.

Getting there turns out to be a major effort. Only one of the originally eight lanes is still navigable, the current is very strong, the water dirty and smelly. Garbage, feces and animal cadavers are floating by; the air carries the sweet scent of decomposition.

People are desperately trying to save their most important belongings in big plastic bowls.

After about one hour the team arrives at the monastery. In order to get in they have to climb a one and a half meters high sandbag wall, then they have another 30 minutes of troublesome path ahead of them. Partially the water has reached chest height. Inside the temple they find a very sad scenario. Even though all cages had been elevated in preparation for the flooding, the waters were merciless, some animals drowned painfully. Many huts have collapsed. Dogs have saved themselves to higher grounds like roofs and trees, many have deep cuts or infected injuries from the sharp roofs.

The path to the temple where the animals have stranded is hard.

Walking becomes impossible; the only way to move forward is by swimming. The sun sets and countless hungry mosquitoes arise carrying dengue and other dangerous diseases. However, the volunteers keep moving forward. They hear miserable whining coming from a nearby shed. Debris, garbage and feces are floating in front of the shed; the volunteers have to dive underneath it in order to get in. On an area of about two by three meters a pack of dogs has taken refuge on top of a few cabinets – the last dry spots.

Even styrofoam boxes come to the rescue...

The animals are grateful for food and clean water, but they do not want to be touched. Most of them are petrified of humans, due to their abusive past. Catching these poor creatures becomes a challenging task. It needs experience, strength and speed. After being caught the animals are put into foam boxes or small boats and are brought to dry grounds via the same troublesome route.

Finally, they arrive at the dry shelter, the second floor of a vacant factory building. Their health and medical needs are evaluated and they are brought into different halls of the buildings. Their major wounds receive treatment, food and water is provided.

Not only dogs are happy about the dry and save shelter, there are people, chickens, cats, pigs and several other creatures, all grateful for a night on dry grounds. Their social behavior is amazing, the atmosphere very peaceful. Those who are suffering from breed specific legislation elsewhere, such as Rottweilers and Pitbulls to name only a few, are co-existing peacefully with all other two and four-legged evacuees. They do not have any problem with one another.

At nine p.m. the volunteers have to return to Bangkok. The water on the roads has risen further;

the flooded lanes can hardly be seen. Count of the day: 200 animals have been rescued, however, many had to be left behind. After the exhausting trip the helpers are hungry and thirsty, are looking forward to a shower. Nobody knows if this is still possible at home, maybe the water in their houses has already reached the ceiling. If not – all agree- they will continue their efforts to rescue as many animals as possible.

Lisa and Phillip are lucky, most of their friends, too. Their house is still relatively dry.

The evacuation of the temple can go on.

After several days of hard work and fight against water and sun, finally a success: All dogs and cats could be rescued, the animals have found shelter, medical care is provided, food and water available.

Other volunteers are helping with the cleaning of the building.

Time to take a deep breath.

Baby is reading the news of the ongoing rescue efforts in Thailand.

Baby listens to music

Baby's two legged mom is relieved, sinks into the couch and tries to relax. The best way to clear her head is by listening to music. Classical music. Mozart.

"Poor dog" , Baby's owner is told frequently, "it must be horrible for those sensitive dog ears" . If Baby's owner had been faced with this accusation, before the dog had the first contact with Mozart, she might have believed it. Well, and probably Baby would never have found her most favorite hobby.

Baby is different. Unique and special. Baby does enjoy listening to Mozart, Beethoven and others.

Going for a walk, running freely in nature? Well, if human thinks so, she can do it. On her own, with friends, with a walking group or with any other masochist. But certainly not with innocent bulldogs having tiny, sensitive paws. Furthermore, bulldogs are very vulnerable and susceptible to extreme weather conditions. Drizzle, fog, wind, sun – so many things that could happen when leaving the house for more than ten meters. Possibly the sky might fall on one's head!

"Can somebody please contact the local animal rights activists?"

But somehow mom seems to be pitiless. Even though there are so many other nice things she could offer. For example in the first floor, the room with the perfectly bulldog-shaped, comfy sofa and the shelf with these flat, round and shiny things which she puts in the box-thing frequently.

Oh yes, this is the place where life is worth living. On this sofa the small Bully seems to become two *meters long and to take root. The ears change into radars when Mozart comes out of the speakers. Her eyes are closed half way, her head is resting on mom's lap not moving before the last note fades. Then she sometimes sits down in front of the speakers hoping the music could start all over again.*

Whoever might think Baby Balou does not care about the playlist is wrong! Baby has her preferences. She prefers the piano to everything else. A big orchestra is always welcome, too. The order is Mozart, Beethoven, Chopin. Mahler took her a little while to get used to, but now it is fine as well. Only Wagner is not so her favorite. Then even the most laid-back bulldog will move voluntarily and vanish into another room.

Luckily, mom has understanding today. After the anxiety about her friends in Bangko, mom is playing Baby's most favorite music. Piano concert in C

Major. Written by Wolfgang Amadeus. Baby is absolultely sure: The andante was just written for French Bulldogs.

Foundling

Meanwhile in Bangkok the rescue workers are having a cold beer at their neighborhood corner. Switch off and relax.

However, rescue workers seem to have a note engraved on their foreheads: Dogs in need, welcome!

Lisa and Phillip are just about to take the first sip, when a panic-stricken flash passes them. It runs down the road and is suddenly stopped by a pack of soidogs – the Beagle Boys say hi. So, u-turning and taking another flight in the other direction in order to be immediately stopped by the next k9-gang. The puppy is trapped and desperately surrenders in the middle of the junction.

The beer gets warm. Lisa gets up and finds her way through the traffic to the pursued pup. Without any resistance he allows her to pick him up and gratefully curls on her lap. He spends the night in a doggy crate. The small boy is well groomed and obviously used to being around humans. However, he is very tired and confused. Probably his owners had planned to evacuate him as well, but somehow on the way he got loose and lost. Nobody knows him here.

Maybe his owners are looking for him, maybe they were forced to abandon him due to the flooding? What to do with him?

Well, in the next morning Lisa and the little fluffy fur ball are riding on a motorbike taxi heading to a temporary emergency dog rescue center on the other side of town. There he will be looked after well and will have time to feed up.

It would be nice to locate his owners. If they cannot be found, Phillip will try to re-home him to a friend in Germany, and well, if anything else fails...

Evacuation

At the moment the paws of Tequila, Ginger and the rest of the pack are still somewhat dry, thanks to the pump at home. However, there are some problems with a dam and slowly but constantly the water is inundating Lak si. The Germans in Bangkok have to think about evacuating, too. They need to find dog-friendly shelter. And they are succesful - thanks to their dog-loving friends.

While people in their home in Upper Franconia are celebrating the All Saints day with calm autumn weather evacuation routes are being prepared in Thailand. Next morning, very early, Lisa and Phillip want to set off. Before that the last moveable belongings have to be moved upstairs to the first floor, the last desperate attempts to seal off the property are made. It would be good to sleep for some hours before leaving.

No chance. The water keeps rising, faster and faster. Almost one foot within an hour. To keep waiting could be fatal. They have to go and get the car which is parked on a bridge. Supplies and the most important documents need to be packed into it. All this is happening in the dark, since the electricity supply has already collapsed.

The car is turning into some kind of ark. Lisa and Phillip are sharing the ride with a neighbor who was cut off by the waters, seven dogs and one cat. They start a journey with uncertain ending.

The truck turns into an ark.

Hitting the road

The arterial road has already turned into a stream, several major roads had to be closed. However, turning back is not possible, the only escape is forward, an uncertain voyage through the night.

Somehow the small group manages to reach the house of their neighbor`s parents. His entire family has gathered there in order to evacuate together, get away from the flooding. Despite their common problems the atmosphere is relaxed, everybody is extremely helpful. Lisa and Phillip, however, are again facing new challenges: The shelter they were aiming for is no longer available – it is flooded, too.

Bangkok`s roads have turned into streams.

Only one option is left. The ark-truck has to serve as an emergency shelter for the night, for two humans, seven dogs and one cat. Then an emergency call has to be made hoping to find a dry place to stay.

Even after more than 2,000 years the quest for shelter is still successful. The owner of a plantation in Sa Keao province is willing to take humans and animals in. A tent is set up, the newcomers are warmly welcomed and well cared for. There is no electricity available but there is a generator to get some clean water up from a nearby pond.

Continuing their studies is not possible for Lisa and Phillip at the moment. Postgraduate studies will have to wait for a while. Yet, nobody is thinking about taking a rest, lying back or dolce vita. There is an internet café a few miles down the bumpy road, it can be used to help other animals in need. Relationships with the home country are maintained, connections to journalists are made in order to remind of the situation around the official media reports and to ask for donations for those in desperate need.

Looks like camping-holidays, it is not...

What might sound like a great adventure to outsiders is hard reality, in fact. Will the stranded ones be able to return to their home? How long will the robinsonade continue? And, especially, what does the own home look like?

The evacuees fear that termites might have moved into the wooden parts of the structure. Mosquitoes might be breeding happily inside their house and scorpions looking for a dry spot to hide. Furthermore, several snake and crocodile farms have been flushed away. Several crocodiles have been spotted in the district Lak si, and the highly poisonous green mambas seem to have plans to start a new population there.

Camp Robinson

Not exactly a five-star accommodation, but they are all safe in Camp Robinson.

Humans and animals are trying to get used to their new home in Camp-Robinson.

Ming Ming the cat does not consider the exceptional situation, she maintains her noble and elegant calmness and demands that her needs are being met. A real diva.

Tequila the black French bulldog, Baby Balou`s mom, has found her way to get accustomed to her new life. Sleeping in, getting body-rubs and not to forget her most favorite hobby: the nearby pond perfectly suits for daily swimming exercises.

Tequila focuses on the positive things, she uses the nearby pond for her daily workouts.

Baby`s sister Ginger is not very keen on swimming and would rather go and look for some game; unfortunately, Ginger`s owners think otherwise.

Massimo is macho. Cane Corso. He meets all cliché of a real Italian, hot-tempered and self-confident. But: in female hands like wax. Whatever mom wants, he does it. Unconditionally, subito, without any complaints.

The perfect guardian for the small group.

Massimo taking a nap

Leki is young, rambunctious and well equipped with one hundred thousand volt-power and countless fancy ideas in her small head. The Malinois-girly keeps everybody busy. She does not even fancy that things could get boring during this catastrophe.

Emma likes the idea of adding some plastics to her diet, and this delicious thought drives her to scout for some special treats on her own. Phillip is looking for Emma. He meets a farmer, who believes to have seen a ridgeback. His first thought was that it would be a dog from the village, but he immediately changes his mind pointing to something on the ground and saying: "No Thai-dog would ever eat this...." Whatever Emma might have snacked - after a little while she comes back to the camp, happy and satisfied.

The two evacuated soidogs Sonnenschein and Windhund are facing entirely new challenges. Suddenly all the freedom has gone and one has to learn to walk on a leash and to accept the fact that one has to be tied up. No big deal. Walking on a leash is done within ten minutes and the idea of being tied up next to the truck is no problem. After all, this was their most favorite spot to sleep back in Lak si, virtually a mobile home.

The truck is turning into a caravan.

Baby is hungry

Speaking of food. Actually, Baby is directly related to Tequila and Ginger but when it comes to food, she rather takes Emma`s site. Anything that can be chewed is considered to be food. No exception! Well, not everything, bananas are yukky, these are disdained vehemently. Anything else can be crammed. If only mom would not be watching so closely all the time. Too bad. One misses all the good things.

Sister Pepper in Upper Franconia is much better off. She is allowed to eat loads. But she does not want to. She pays a lot of attention to her bikini body. Nobody knows why, because for Pepper swimming is as unpopular as for Baby, thus she could strike unrestrained.

So, what to do when the size of the black hole in one`s own tummy starts competing with the one in outer space? When an additional treat becomes as important as the air to breathe? Baby remembers that the unloved walkies, when they took place even under hard resistance, always brought some reward. Well! Let`s check out the kitchen. Sit, down, ⋯the entire program. Making big eyes and looking at mom in a heart rendering way.

Nothing! Unbelievable! Mom thinks that the post-walky-jerky, at least five minutes ago, should be sufficient.

Two minutes later. Baby tiptoes to mom. Nudges her with her nose, rushes to the backyard door and comes back.

No response.

Again. Nudging, backyard door, sit in front of mom.

Negative.

One more time! Nudging, backyard door. "Fiep! Wooff! Fiiiieeeep! "

Finally. Human shows understanding. Opens the door. Baby seems desperate to get out one more time. Long live a backyard.

Tapp, tapp, tapp. Squatting down... to pretend as if!

Full speed back into the kitchen. Sit in front of the goody-box. "Well, mom? Did you see how nicely I did toilet in the garden? Where is my reward?"

So much sophistication weakens even the strictest mom.

Ginger is sick

Even though the situation is new and unfamiliar to everybody, all are settling in quite well in Camp Robinson. But, how is the saying: nothing is so bad that things could not get worse.

All of a sudden Ginger gets depressed. All washed out and exhausted. Her temperature gets very high. Where is the next vet clinic? Finding a vet with good reputation on the countryside is a difficult up to impossible task. What to do? What is wrong with the doggy?

The symptoms suggest tick borne blood-parasites. Lisa knows this disease from her work as an animal activist. But is the suspicion correct? There is no lab available. No time to think about it any longer. If caught early, these pests can be treated quite well with antibiotics, if left untreated, they are usually fatal. Something must be done. Now. An antibiotic is necessary. Even though the evacuation was done in a hurry, with only the most essential belongings, some drugs can be found.

Lisa`s guts were right. It does not take long and Ginger is doing much better.

After three long weeks the time comes when one can start to think about returning home.

The return

Striking the tent, fitting the few left belongings back into the truck, aboard the animals – this is done in no time.

However, the way back will not turn out as a pleasant Sunday afternoon walk.

Even on the way back humans and animals have to fight the water.

Traffic jam. One single road to and from Bangkok has mostly been spared and is somewhat navigable. The smaller ones that have to be used in order to get home are covered with algae and slippery. Even with 30 degree Celsius in the tropics they resemble icy roads in Upper Franconia which ran out of salt. From time to time animal cadavers are floating by. The animal activists are heartbroken.

The group gradually fights its way forward, meter by meter. Finally, they are warmly welcomed by their neighbors. Some of them have already returned to Lak si and started working: keeping the gullies clean and pumping remaining water from lower lying properties and houses.

The own garden has turned into a puddle of mud, not a single piece of lawn is left, only a few large plants have survived. But how to get into the house? The wooden door is swollen so badly that tools would be necessary to open it. Tools which are inside the house. A security door is locked with a padlock. But where is the key? It is probably doing some swimming exercises in the floods.

Luckily, Lisa is slim and athletic. And the house has a doggy-door. The only option to get inside is to crawl through dirt, soil, and water which is 15 centimeters high.

The view is devastating. The sewer has gone over, the water in bathroom and kitchen is still up to the knees and the walls in the living room clearly show the water levels. The entire kitchen can no longer be used. Walls and ceilings are covered with thousands of hungry mosquitoes. What used to be bright and white has turned grayish-black. The smell inside the house remembers of harbor and sewage. Thinking of living there is by far not possible.

But in Thailand nobody gives up. The mud must be removed, the pests exterminated and the houses need to be cleaned thoroughly. In fact, the two Germans are not only concerned about the well being of animals but also about conservation and environmental compatibility. However, bringing this place back to a place worth living in - for humans and animals - chemicals are ineluctable. Whereby the next challenge arises. Many households are dealing with the same problems like Lisa and Phillip, appliances are scarce and hard to obtain. But problems are there to be solved.

This means rubbing the walls with disinfectants and getting rid of the entire kitchen furniture. A big hose with high pressure is necessary in order to flush the dirt and soil out of the house. Then the pump is needed again to get rid of water, soil, bacteria and other contaminants. The to-do-list seems to be like a never ending story. Everything in the first floor that was spared by the flood has to be carried downstairs again. The neighbor's valuables that were stored there as well need to be returned. And, and, and...

Anyhow, everybody remains relaxed following the teaching of the monk of a Nonthaburi Temple: "Let the water flood your house. Don't let your mind get flooded with suffering!"

Meanwhile Ming Ming and the doggies have settled in well in their own home again. Sonnenschein and Windhund who are usually happy with their outdoor-freedom get comfy with the pillows in the bed. But soon they are eager to explore their neighborhood and all the changes the waters have brought. Excellent! The garbage has not been collected for weeks. And all houses are being mucked out. Elation! First extensive wallowing in the irresistible scents, then the hunt for goodies can start. For sure, some great toys or even carelessly thrown away food will be out there. Plundering garbage cans becomes their new most favorite hobby.

Well, apparently the little fluffy fur ball is still there, in the emergency shelter. Lisa wants to visit him the following morning and prepares some posters for pet-shops and vet clinics. If he cannot be reunited with his original owners, Phillip would take care of re-homing him to Germany, and if nobody wants to adopt him, there is a house with open doors in Lak si.

Besides all the necessary renovations and clean up efforts and the by now started classes at university phones and e-mails are not quiescent. So far many dogs have been reunited with their owners or re-homed to new families, others, however, still need some basic training before being ready for adoption. And since Lisa has the right touch with dogs, she is also taking this responsibility. Unsalaried! She does not think about money, all she cares about is preparing the dogs for their new families and providing some fundamental basic training.

Puppy

Ayutthaya. City of kings. And of waters. Flood-waters.

Like anywhere else dogs are fighting for survival there: soidogs, dogs abandoned by force, big and small ones, old and young ones. And unborn ones. The waters were irrespective. Puppies are born during crisis, too. The flooding makes their start into life even more difficult as it would be anyway. It is so sad if you only see cages and fencing of the emergency shelter as light of the day.

Nevertheless, Aughiski is lucky. Very lucky. His mom and five littermates are doing well and are lovingly looked after. At the moment. If one is planning to turn into a Great Dane, the prospects for being adopted by a fond family with a suitable home are not the brightest ones.

But there are still Lisa, Phillip and the big doggy-family in Lak si. Over there they are still a little bit sad, not only because of the damages left by the flood but also because "Captain General" known as the Great Dane "Kuhn Pol" had passed away shortly before the flood hit. What would be closer than adopting a Great Dane puppy?

Unfortunately, the human-parents were not really able to care for a puppy while they were staying in Camp Robinson, they could only hope to find the puppy alive and kicking after returning.

Finally the big day for the small boy is coming. He is picked up, and with nine weeks of age he is allowed to move in with his new family. This changes his life. Completely. There are so many things to do and explore. Eating, playing, sleeping, the puppy's schedule is full. A real Great Dane does not bother and settles in within a new time-record.

The lucky one: Great Dane Aughiski has a new home.

Back to day-to-day-life

Fright and backing down are not an option. After all, problems are only there to be solved. This means to continue cleaning and tidying, renovating, buying new furniture, looking after the garden.

Schools and universities have re-opened, and slowly routine comes back to day-today life.

The animal welfare work gets back to normal and is continued as usual. After the flooding there is more than enough work that needs to be done.

Oh yes, the little fluffy fur ball which was rescued shortly before the evacuation. Actually, everybody hoped to find his original owners or to re-home the small boy. With one option. If anything else fails...

And that's the turn it takes: "Dogs in need welcome".

The little fluffy fur ball is renamed to Chester and gets the new best friend and housemate of Dane Aughiski and Tequila and Ginger and Massimo and Leki and Emma and Windhund and Sonnenschein and Ming Ming...